Level 3

THIS WALKER BOOK BELONGS TO:

Rub-a-dub-dub,
Three men in a tub,
And how do you think they got there?
The butcher, The baker, The candlestick-maker?
They all jumped out of a rotten potato.
'T'was enough to make a man stare.
Peter, Peter, pumpkin eater,
Had a wife and couldn't keep her,
He put her in a pumpkin shell
And there he kept her very well.
MOTHERGOOSEVILLE

There was an old woman who lived in a shoe,
She had so many children she didn't know what to do;
She gave them some broth without any bread;
She whipped them all soundly and put them to bed.

Toni Goffe

JOE GIANT'S MISSING BOOT

A Mothergooseville Story

WALKER BOOKS
LONDON

To Tim
who likes a nice giant

First published 1990 by Walker Books Ltd
87 Vauxhall Walk, London SE11 5HJ

This edition published 1991
Reprinted 1992, 1993

Printed and bound in Hong Kong by
Sheck Wah Tong Printing Press Ltd

British Library Cataloguing in Publication Data
Goffe, Toni
Joe Giant's missing boot.
I. Title
823'.914 [J]
ISBN 0-7445-2050-9

Once upon a time, Joe Giant and his wife, Tilda, came to live in Mothergooseville.

"I like it here," said Tilda, "but a new home needs new friends. What we must do now is get to know our neighbours."

Early next morning, Tilda took Joe a cup of tea in bed.

"Time to get up!" she shouted in his ear. For someone so little, Tilda had a very loud voice and Joe woke up at once.

He dressed and pulled on one of his boots. He looked round for the other.

"I can't find my boot," he called.

"Well, I haven't got it," snapped Tilda. "I expect you lost it on the way here. You'd better go and have a look after breakfast."

So Joe ate his breakfast and hopped off down the road to find his boot.

"Don't forget to make friends!" Tilda called after him. She was a little worried because giants are rather clumsy and sometimes they upset people.

Peter Peter, the pumpkin eater, was looking for his wife. Though he had a pumpkin patch, he had no house, so his wife had wandered off to find a place to live. Peter Peter missed her very much.

"Hello!" said Joe Giant, hopping up behind him and making him jump. "Have you seen my boot?"

"No, I haven't. Have you seen my wife?"

"I'm afraid not."

"That's that, then," Peter Peter sighed. He looked down at his pumpkin patch. "Hey, you're squashing my pumpkins!"

"Oops, I'm sorry," said Joe. "Oh dear."

Joe's sock was now all sticky with pumpkin juice, so he hopped down to the sea and washed it.

"I'll have a swim while it dries," he thought, and dived under the water to see how far he could go without taking a breath.

He held on as long as he could and then came to the surface with a great whoooosssh! Feeling rather pleased with himself, he headed back to the shore.

As he was dressing, three wet figures crawled out of the water spluttering furiously. It was the butcher, the baker and the candlestick maker.

"You sank our tub, you clumsy idiot!" they shouted.

"I'm sorry, I didn't see you," said Joe apologetically. "Oh dear, and I still haven't found my boot..."

"Did you say 'boot'?" asked the butcher. "How extraordinary! I've just seen a huge boot. I saw it when you tossed us up in the air. It's over that hill."

Joe beamed. "Oh, good! I must go and get it, but I'll be back."

He hopped up the hill and peered over. There stood his missing boot! But something was wrong. The boot looked different. Suddenly he realized what it was – there was smoke coming out of the top! Someone had built a roof with a chimney, and cut windows and a door in the sides.

Quite forgetting what Tilda had said about making friends, Joe stomped over to the boot and roared, "Fee fi fo foot, who's living in my boot?"

The ground shook like an earthquake as the door of the boot opened and out poured more children than he could count.

With them came an old woman angrily waving a stick.

"What do you mean by frightening my children?" she shouted.

"What do you mean by living in my boot?" roared Joe.

At this, the old woman stopped being angry and began to cry.

"I've got so many children," she sobbed, "I don't know what to do. I was very pleased to find your boot, but even that's not big enough. The children are all squashed up..."

Joe felt very ashamed of himself. He thought hard for a moment, then he had an idea.

"I know! You can have my other boot as well. Then there'll be enough room for everyone."

"Oh, thank you!" cried the old woman, and the children cheered.

Joe played with the children for a while. They ran all over him, slid down his legs and bounced on his tummy.

"Well, I suppose I'd better be going," he said at last. Just then, something caught his eye. "What a big pumpkin! Would you let

me have it – and its wooden tub – in exchange for my boot?"

"Of course," said the old woman.

"Thank you," said Joe.

"Thank *you*!" called the children. "No more awful pumpkin broth!"

Joe went back to the beach where the butcher, the baker and the candlestick maker were sitting sadly on the sand. He gave them the tub.

"Thank you, Joe, it's perfect!" they said, and they jumped in at once.

Then he went to Peter Peter's pumpkin patch.

"Could you and your wife make a house out of this great pumpkin?" he asked.

"Why, yes, I believe we could," said Peter Peter, and a big smile spread over his face. "That should keep us very well!"

When Joe got home, he started to tell Tilda about his adventures.

"What!" she burst out. "You trampled Peter Peter's pumpkins, upset the three men in a tub, and gave away your other boot? I'm so cross with you!"

"But I haven't told you what happened next," said Joe.

"I won't listen to another word," Tilda snapped. "And you can go to bed without any supper."

Joe tramped sadly upstairs. Just then there was a knock at the door. It was the old woman who lived in a shoe.

"Can I come in?" she asked, and she told Tilda everything Joe had done that day.

"To thank him for being so kind, we've asked the cobbler to make him a new pair of boots," she added. "And now, goodbye. I'm sure we're going to be great friends."

When the old woman had gone, Tilda hurried to the kitchen and made Joe a huge plate of spaghetti and cheese on toast – his favourite. She carried it carefully upstairs.

"I was wrong about you, dear, and I'm sorry," she said. "That nice old woman who lives in your boots has explained everything."

And she sat by Joe as he munched his spaghetti, smiling at the thought of all their new friends.

MOTHERGOOSEVILLE

MORE WALKER PAPERBACKS
For You to Enjoy

CLAP YOUR HANDS / STAMP YOUR FEET

by Sarah Hayes/Toni Goffe

Two collections of favourite action rhymes, with detailed step-by-step illustrations.
"Jolly rhymes... Lively, friendly illustrations." *Books for Keeps*

ISBN 0-7445-1231-X *Clap Your Hands* £3.99
ISBN 0-7445-1232-8 *Stamp Your Feet* £3.99

MING LO MOVES THE MOUNTAIN

by Arnold Lobel

Included on the original list of Level 3 texts to be used in conjunction with the Standard Assessment Tasks of the National Curriculum, this is the entertaining story of a man's efforts to move the mountain that towers over his house – by one of the greatest ever children's picture book creators.

ISBN 0-7445-2179-3 £3.99

SHAKER LANE

by Alice and Martin Provensen

Also an approved Level 3 text, this is a thoughtful account of a changing rural landscape and its inhabitants.
"The Provensens are masters of their art."
Dorothy Butler, Babies Need Books

ISBN 0-7445-2098-3 £3.99

Walker Paperbacks are available from most booksellers, or by post from Walker Books Ltd, PO Box 11, Falmouth, Cornwall TR10 9EN.

To order, send:
Title, author, ISBN number and price for each book ordered
Your full name and address
Cheque or postal order for the total amount, plus postage and packing:

UK and BFPO Customers – £1.00 for first book, plus 50p for the second book and plus 30p for each additional book to a maximum charge of £3.00.
Overseas and Eire Customers – £2.00 for first book, plus £1.00 for the second book and plus 50p per copy for each additional book.
Prices are correct at time of going to press, but are subject to change without notice.